Kate had a dog.
Kate and the dog had
to take a bus to get
home.

Kate and the dog got on the bus.
Kate gave the man a dime.

The man did not take
the dime.
"The dog can not ride
on the bus," said the
man.

"I can get a big bag,"
said Kate.
"A dog in a bag will
ride on the bus."

The dog was not big.
It fit in the bag.

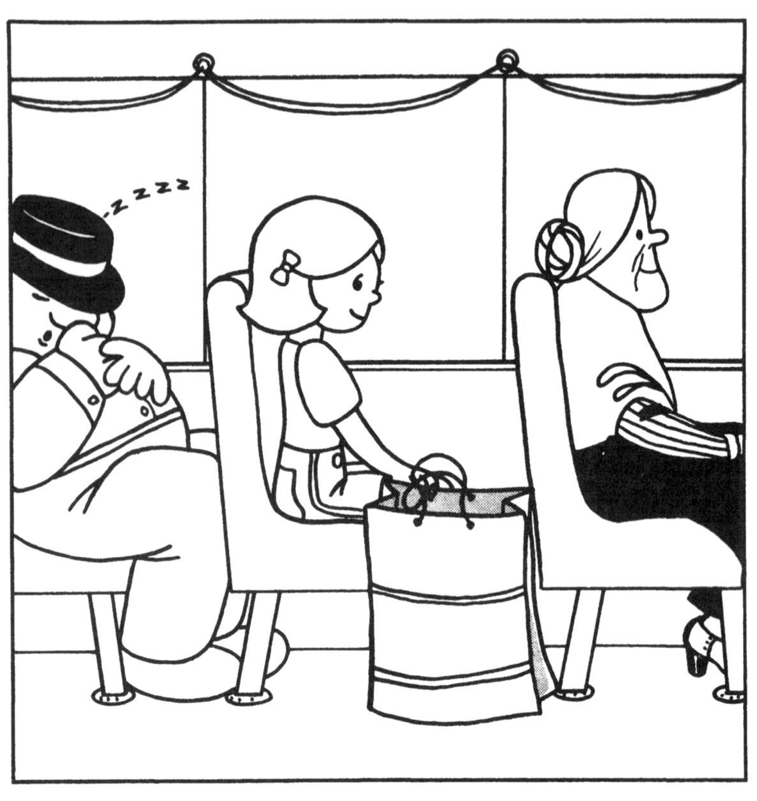

The bus came.
Kate got on the bus
with the bag.

The dog made a hole
in the bag.
The dog put his nose
in the hole.

The dog made the
bag rip.
"Get in the bag,"
said Kate.
But the dog ran.

A big man had a nap.
The dog got up on
his lap.

The man woke up.
He was mad at Kate
and the dog.

A man in a hat had
a cone.
The dog got up on
his lap and had a bit
of the cone.

The man did not like
the dog in his lap.
The cone got on his hat.

It was not wise to take
a dog on the bus.
Kate and the dog did
not get a ride home
on the bus.

It was late and Kate
was sad.
It was a five-mile hike
to get home.

Mom came at a fine time.
Mom gave Kate and
the dog a ride home.

Kate and the dog had
a fine ride.
"I will not take a dog
on the bus," said Kate.
"It is not fun."